WING
GAS
FILL-R-UP
OIL

BIG RIG

By JAMIE A. SWENSON
Pictures by NED YOUNG

DISNEY • HYPERION / Los Angeles New York

For the amazing readers and the children's staff (past, present, & future)
of the Hedberg Public Library in Janesville, Wisconsin
—J.A.S.

For Melanie, my lifelong road-trip partner
—N.Y.

First Edition
10 9 8 7 6 5 4 3 2
FAC-029191-18030

Printed in Malaysia

Reinforced binding
Visit www.DisneyBooks.com

ACKNOWLEDGMENTS

A huge thank-you to Lisl, Ann, Pam, Georgia, Judy, and Elizabeth for loving it, Sean for believing in it—and to Rotem and Hayley for making it come to life. *URRRRNNNT-URRRRNNNT!*
—J.A.S.

With much appreciation to Rotem Moscovich, Hayley Wagreich, and Tyler Nevins, for their excellent navigation skills.
—N.Y.

Library of Congress Cataloging-in-Publication Data

Swenson, Jamie.
Big rig / by Jamie Swenson ; illustrated by Ned Young.—First edition.
pages cm
Summary: Frankie, an eighteen-wheel, semi-truck invites the reader to join him on a job, introducing the work, mechanics, and terminology of trucking along the way.
ISBN 978-1-4231-6330-5—ISBN 1-4231-6330-3
[1. Tractor trailers—Fiction.] I. Young, Ned, illustrator. II. Title.
PZ7.S97488358Big 2014
[E]—dc23 2013012223

Hello there.

Name's Frankie.

Proud to meet you.

I'm a big rig, a semitruck—I've got eighteen ready-to-roll tires just waiting to hit the pavement.

Count 'em and weep:

2, 4, 6, 8,

10, 12, 14, 16, 18.

I’ve got a big job to do—

climb in, you can come too.

We’ve got cargo ready to roll.

What's cargo?

Why, that's what we're carrying.

It could be anything.

You name it, we haul it.

Do I have a horn? Ha!
What do you think?
Go ahead:
pull down—
URRRRNNNT-
URRRRNNNT!

Want to hear that again?
Thought so—
URRRRNNNT—
URRRRNNNT!

I have high-powered, air-pressured, compression brakes.
When I slow, believe me—you'll know.
Go ahead, hit the Jake Brake.
EEEEERRRRRRRRRR...
DAA-DAA-DAA-DA-DA

Well done!
But it's time for the real fun. Let's roll.

Rain clouds? Not a problem.

Wipers—do your job—

SCHWAAT,
SCHWAAT,
SCHWAAT

Lights on—can't miss me, I'm a Christmas tree.

Looks like blue skies on the horizon.

We go full throttle—

Folks wave hello— Right back at you.

We pass kiddie cars, Beetles, and land yachts.

Do you think they want to hear our horn?

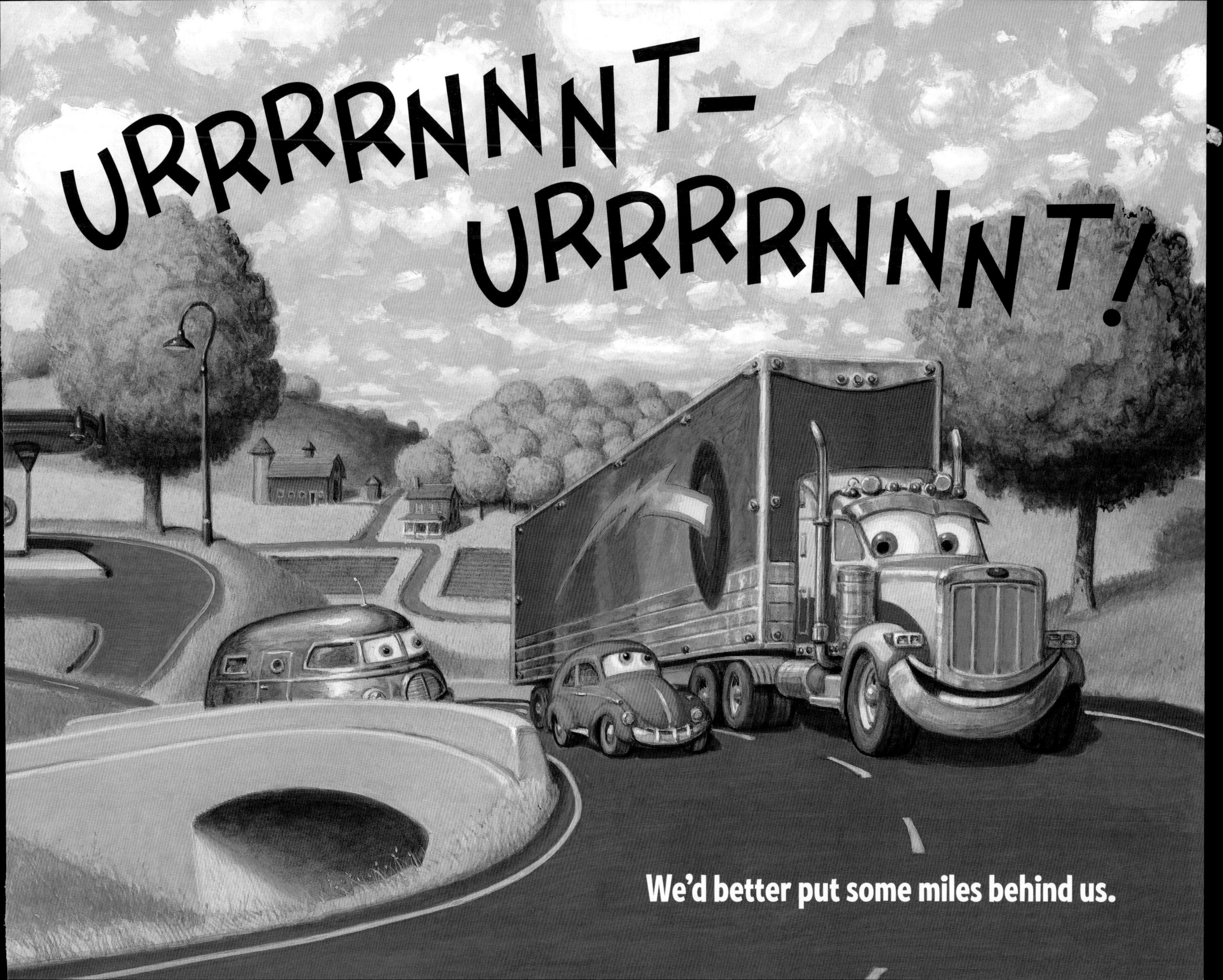
URRRRNNNT–
URRRRNNNNT!
We’d better put some miles behind us.

BANG

POP

SSSSSSSSSSHHHHHHHHHH

UUUUUUUUUUUUU

Oh no!
A blowout!

Back off the hammer!
Hit the brake!
Use the Jake!

Alligators everywhere!

Look right! Hold tight!

Swerve left.

WHOAAA—

Pull over!
EEEEERRRRRRRRRRR. . .
DAA-DAA-DAA-DA-DA

Now what? Why, that's easy.
Now
we
wait . . .

for the service truck, who saves the day—

we're all patched up and on our way.

No time to lose—**let's roll.**

We made it—the magic mile.

Way to go!

We’re a hardworking team, you and me.

Catch you on the flip-flop—

Keep the shiny side up and the rubber side down.

URRRRNNNT—
URRRRNNNT!

Truck-tionary

Alligator: Tread from an eighteen-wheeler in the road

Back off the hammer: Slow down/hit the brakes

Beetles: Volkswagen Beetles

Cargo: The freight, or transported goods, that the truck carries

Christmas tree: Semi with a lot of extra running lights

Flip-flop: Return trip

Full throttle: Maximum speed

Kiddie cars: School buses

Land yachts: Mobile homes

Magic mile: Final mile of any trip

Service truck: Tow truck/vehicle sent to fix up big rigs

Shiny side up and rubber side down: Be careful

Use the Jake: Hit the brakes (Jake Brake/Jacobs Brake is a brand of compression brakes)

FLEET
WING
GAS
FILL-R-UP
OIL